JUDY MOODY
GIRL DETECTIVE

Books by Megan McDonald and Peter H. Reynolds

Judy Moody
Judy Moody Gets Famous!
Judy Moody Saves the World!
Judy Moody Predicts the Future
Judy Moody: The Doctor Is In!
Judy Moody Declares Independence!
Judy Moody: Around the World in 8½ Days
Judy Moody Goes to College
Judy Moody, Girl Detective
Judy Moody and the NOT Bummer Summer
Judy Moody and the Bad Luck Charm
Judy Moody, Mood Martian
Judy Moody and the Bucket List
Judy Moody and the Right Royal Tea Party
Stink: The Incredible Shrinking Kid
Stink and the Incredible Super-Galactic Jawbreaker
Stink and the World's Worst Super-Stinky Sneakers
Stink and the Great Guinea Pig Express
Stink: Solar System Superhero
Stink and the Ultimate Thumb-Wrestling Smackdown
Stink and the Midnight Zombie Walk
Stink and the Freaky Frog Freakout
Stink and the Shark Sleepover
Stink and the Attack of the Slime Mould
Stink: Hamlet and Cheese
Stink-O-Pedia: Super Stink-y Stuff from A to Zzzzz
Stink-O-Pedia 2: More Stink-y Stuff from A to Z
Judy Moody & Stink: The Holly Joliday
Judy Moody & Stink: The Mad, Mad, Mad, Mad Treasure Hunt
Judy Moody & Stink: The Big Bad Blackout
Judy Moody & Stink: The Wishbone Wish

Books by Megan McDonald

The Sisters Club • *The Sisters Club: Rule of Three*
The Sisters Club: Cloudy with a Chance of Boys

Books by Peter H. Reynolds

The Dot • *Ish* • *So Few of Me* • *Sky Colour*

MEGAN McDONALD

illustrated by Peter H. Reynolds

JUDY MOODY

GIRL DETECTIVE

WALKER
BOOKS

First published 2011 by Walker Books Ltd
87 Vauxhall Walk, London SE11 5HJ

This edition published 2019

2 4 6 8 10 9 7 5 3 1

British Library Cataloguing in Publication Data:
a catalogue record for this book
is available from the British Library

ISBN 978-1-4063-9229-6

www.walker.co.uk

For Jordan and Chloe
M. M.

To Marlo Thomas and Carole Hart,
who have inspired all of us to be "free to be".
P. H. R.

Table of Contents

Who's

JuDY MOODY

Agent Liz Inkwell,
aka Judy Drewdy,
World's Best Mystery Solver
(WBMS)

Dad

Father of WBMS

MuM

Mother of WBMS

StinK

Agent James Madagascar

Who

Rocky
Agent Spuds Houdini

Frank
Agent Dills Pickle

Officer Kopp
Crime Prevention Guru

Mr Chips
K-9 Detective-in-Training

The Case of the Bothersome Brother

It was a dark and stormy night. Rain slashed the window. Lightning flashed and thunder crashed. Spooky shadows like giant teeth danced across the walls.

Tick-tock, tick-tock went the old clock, thumping like a scary heartbeat. Quiet as a ghost, she climbed the dark, dark stairs. In her bare feet, she tiptoed down the dark, dark hallway to the dark, dark door.

She tapped <u>one, two, three</u> *times, signalling in Morse code. Just then, the* <u>door</u> *creaked open.*

Knock-knock.

"AAHHH!" screamed Judy from under the covers of her top bunk bed. She let go of the Mood Libs notepad she'd been writing in. It sailed through the air, hitting Stink on the head.

"Ouch!" yelled Stink, rubbing his head. "Watch the brains! You're gonna give me an egg on my head."

"You already are an egghead, Stink," Judy teased.

"Well, you didn't have to throw the book at me."

"At least it wasn't the encyclopedia.

That's what you get for scaring me silly while I was writing a spooky Mood Libs story."

"Why are you under the covers? It's the middle of the day."

"Nancy Drew says a person should never be afraid of the dark. So I was practising."

"Why do you have a torch?"

"A good detective always keeps a torch under her pillow."

"Does Nancy Drew do that?"

"Hel-*lo*! Haven't you read *The Message in the Hollow Oak*?"

"I'm not a Nancy Drew cuckoo-head like some people!"

"Can I help it if I'm trying to read all

fifty-six original Nancy Drew classics?"

Stink waved the Mood Libs book at her. "Does Nancy Drew throw stuff at her brother, too?"

"Nancy Drew doesn't have a brother. But if she did, I'm sure she'd throw stuff if he scared the jeepers out of her."

"Jeepers?"

"That's Nancy Drew talk, Stink. Get a clue."

"Do Nancy Drew mysteries have any stuff that blows up? Good mysteries have stuff that blows up. Like boats or cakes or maybe exploding motorcycles?"

"No, Stink. Nancy Drew mysteries have old clocks and hidden diaries and squeaky steps and stuff."

"Oh," said Stink. He did not sound one teeny bit scared. He sounded a teeny bit bored.

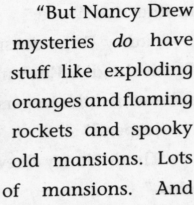

"But Nancy Drew mysteries *do* have stuff like exploding oranges and flaming rockets and spooky old mansions. Lots of mansions. And they are all haunted, and once Nancy Drew almost gets crushed when the ceiling falls on her. Another time she's chased by a phantom horse. She even gets strangled by a giant python. No lie."

"Exploding pythons are cool," said

Stink, getting mixed up. "Can I look at one of your Nancy Drews?"

"Over there." Judy pointed to a pile of stuff on her desk. "Under my sock monkey."

Stink lifted up the sock monkey. "Under your sock monkey is a pillow."

"Under the pillow," Judy told him.

Stink lifted the pillow. "Under your pillow is nothing but a big fat dictionary."

"Under the dictionary."

Stink lifted up the dictionary. "It's a mystery just trying to find your Nancy Drew book." Under the dictionary was Nancy Drew book No.43: *The Mystery of the 99 Steps*. "Why's it under all this stuff?"

"Well, um ... don't laugh, but—"

"Ha! Ju-dy is scare-dy!" Stink chimed. "You hid it under here because it's *scary*. You're scared of a Nancy Drew nightmare!"

"Can I help it if I have an over-achieving imagination?" asked Judy. "I double-dare *you* to read it. *In the dark.*"

Stink shivered.

"See, Nancy's friend has this weird dream about these creepy ninety-nine steps, so Nancy goes to France to try to find them and solve the mystery of her friend's dream. It's spine-chilling. Says so right on the back. Books don't lie, Stink."

"Maybe you'll have a bad dream from reading the book. Then *I* can go to France to solve the mystery of your bad dream ... and see the Eiffel Tower."

"The Eiffel Tower is *so* beside the point, Stink. But you just gave me a genius idea. I'm going to solve a mystery. A real-life, Nancy-Drew, scare-yourself-silly mystery. For sure and absolute positive."

"What's the mystery?"

"I don't know yet. I have to find one first."

"Do you have to go to France to find it?"

"Stink, you don't have to leave the country to find a mystery. There could be one right in your own back garden."

Stink looked out the window into the garden. "All I see out there is your purple skipping rope, a pink-and-white football, your bike with the flat tyre and the blue tent we use for the Toad Pee Club. The only mystery is why Mum and Dad don't make you pick up your stuff."

"Ha, ha. Very funny. A mystery is out there, Stink. Maybe not in the back garden exactly. But it could be right under our noses. All we have to do is pay attention."

Just like that, she, Judy Moody, went looking for a mystery.

The Mystery of the Missing Moose Mice

If a person were going to solve a big fat mystery, she had to have a way-official Nancy Drew detective kit.

Torch? Check.

Notebook? Check.

Grouchy pencil? Check.

Pocket magnifying glass? Check.

Duck tape? Check.

Zip-top bag? Check.

"Let's see," Judy said out loud to herself. "All I need now is a disguise, some money and a French dictionary."

She went into the upstairs bathroom and came back with Mum's make-up bag. Judy pulled out a red lipstick, a compact, an eyebrow pencil, nail polish, tweezers and a kirby grip.

"Ooh, cool," said Stink, coming into her room. "Is all this stuff for a disguise?"

"Stink, don't you know anything about detective work? Everybody knows lipstick is for writing SOS messages."

"Oh, I get it. Like if something explodes and your leg is pinned under a piece of metal, and you go to yell 'help' in French, but you lost your French dictionary, you

23

write *SOS* in red lipstick or something?"

"Or something," said Judy. "Lipstick is good for fake blood, too. Like once, Nancy Drew smeared lipstick on herself and pretended she was bleeding to trick the bad guys so she could escape. There are tons of bad guys, like Snorky, Stumpy, Sniggs and Grumper."

Stink snorted. "They sound like dwarves, not bad guys."

"And in *The Phantom of Pine Hill,* there's an evil fortune-teller named Madame Tarantella."

"Madame Tarantula. Cool. Can I try writing in lipstick?" Stink asked.

"It's only for emergencies, Stink," said Judy.

"What about all that other junk?"

"The powder in the compact can be used to dust for fingerprints, and the little mirror is for spying on somebody. The eyebrow pencil is for this." Judy drew a quick moustache on Stink.

"Hey!" said Stink, but instead of wiping his lip, he looked in the mirror.

Judy held up a little black metal hair clip. "Rule Number One: never leave home without a kirby grip."

"What's a kirby grip?" Stink asked.

"This baby is for picking locks."

"Can I try?"

"Knock yourself out," Judy said, handing him a kirby grip. Judy loaded all the detective stuff into her backpack.

Stink picked up Judy's secret diary, stuck the kirby grip in the keyhole and turned it.

The diary popped open.

"Sweet!" said Stink. "It really works."

Judy looked up. "Give it!" she said, grabbing the diary back.

"Are you sure Nancy Drew doesn't have a little brother? Little brothers make good detectives, too."

"I'm sure. Just a dad named Mr Drew; her two best chums, George and Bess; her dog, Togo; her cat, Snowball; and a shiny blue, way-cool convertible!"

"Nancy Drew is old enough to drive a real car?"

"Tell me about it. Who wouldn't want

to ride around in a convertible solving mysteries all day?" Judy said. "Make-up? Check. There. I'm done!"

"What about the money? Where's the money? You forgot the money!"

"N-no, I didn't."

Stink peered into Judy's backpack and pulled out a plastic bag full of coins.

"Not my state quarters. And my president dollars! I've collected these forever."

"C'mon, Stinker. If I get locked in an attic or a cupboard or the boot of a car, I've got to have some money to bribe the bad guys to let me out."

"Just pick the lock with your kirby grip thingie," said Stink.

Judy shot him a sourball stare.

"Fine!" Stink sorted through his coins. "Here. You can have my American Samoa quarter. Because I don't know where that is."

"One lousy quarter? That's not going to get me un-kidnapped."

"OK! My Martin Van Buren president dollar. But only because he's not James

Madison. And because I don't know who he is."

"Gee, thanks, Stinkerbell."

"Is it time to go and find the mystery now?" asked Stink.

"Almost," said Judy. "I'm hungry. I need a snack. Rule Number One of being a good detective is never solve a mystery on an empty stomach."

"I thought Rule Number One was the kirby grip thing."

"Do you have to listen to everything I say? Stink, turn around so you can't see where I hide my sweets." Stink had found the sweets hidden in her sock drawer. Stink had found the sweets hidden in her doctor kit. Stink had found the sweets hidden in her five hundred-piece puzzle of the Tower of London. But no way would he find the sweets hidden in her double-secret, triple-tricky hiding place.

Stink turned around. He covered his eyes.

"Cover your ears, too," said Judy.

"I only have two hands."

"Try not to listen, then." Judy took out her Build-a-Moose that she had made at the shopping centre with Grandma Lou last Christmas. Judy had filled his tummy with a bag of gummy sweets instead of stuffing. She reached inside and pulled out ... an old striped sock?

"Stink!" said Judy. "You'll never believe what I found."

Stink turned back around and looked. "A sock?" He tried to sound fake-surprised.

"Not just a sock," said Judy. "A sock *and* a mystery. Right here in our own back garden."

Stink did not say a word. Stink stared at the floor.

"A real-life, honest-to-jeepers, Nancy-Drew-who-doesn't-have-any-brothers mystery." Judy waved the sock in the air.

"The Mystery of the Missing Sock?" Stink asked.

"More like the Case of the Stolen Sweets," said Judy. "I hid a bag of gummy sweets in my moose's tummy. But now the sweets are not there. Presto-change-o-gonzo, just like that."

Stink scratched his head. He snapped his fingers. "I bet Mouse got into your moose and ate your mice!"

"Interesting," said Judy. "How did you know they were gummy *mice*, Stink? I said gummy *sweets*. I never said gummy *mice*."

"*Moose. Mouse. Mice.* My tongue got twisted. And I know how much you like those gummy mice. More than gummy eyeballs and gummy frog legs."

"Stink, take off your shoes."

"Huh? Why? But—"

"Just do it."

Stink took off his trainers.

"Aha! Just as I thought! You have odd socks on. And one of the socks you're wearing matches this sock." She held up the striped sock. "The Case of the One-Striped-Sock-Wearing Sweets Stealer is solved. Stink Moody, what do you have to say for yourself?"

"I could really use that lipstick now," said Stink.

"What for?"

"For writing *SOS*. You said that when a person is in trouble, he can use the lipstick for writing *SOS*."

The Secret of the Stolen Spectacles

The next morning, Judy went to Virginia Dare School, third grade, Class 3T, like always. She sat in the second row, like always. Mr Todd started telling Class 3T about the day ahead, like always. Except something was different.

Mr Todd held some paper at arm's length and squinted at it. "We have a special guest coming to school this afternoon," he told them.

Rocky raised his hand. "Mr Todd," he said, "something about you is different today."

Judy turned to look at Rocky and tapped her head as if to say, *ESP. You read my mind!*

"Are you growing a beard?" Rocky asked.

"I'm afraid not," said Mr Todd, scratching his chin.

"You got taller?" said Jordan.

"I don't think so," said Mr Todd.

"You're growing grey hair!" said Bradley.

"You kids *are* giving me a few grey hairs," Mr Todd teased.

Judy looked at Mr Todd. *Something* was different. And she would use her best Nancy Drew super-sleuth amazing detective powers to figure out the Case of the Different Mr Todd.

Judy Moody studied him up, down and sideways, like he was a shiny, wrapped Christmas present. Mr Todd did not have a new tie or a new haircut or new shoes.

Mr Todd leaned on his desk and told the class about the special guest: a policeman named Officer So-and-So and his dog So-and-So, who were coming to school that afternoon to talk about Such and Such. Mr Todd squinted at his paper again.

That's when it hit her. Judy's super-amazing, mystery-solving powers figured out that Mr Todd looked different because he was not wearing his glasses.

"Mr Todd got contacts!" Judy called out.

"I did not get contact lenses," said Mr Todd, squinting at Judy.

Crumbs! Judy had thought she'd cracked the case.

"But I seem to have misplaced my glasses."

Misplaced? Maybe. Lost? Hardly. Mr Todd never took his glasses off. Judy looked around Class 3T. Which kid looked like a third-grade glasses stealer? Bradley? Jordan? Anya? Owen? Jessica Finch, Super-Smart Stellar Speller? Was she the Super-Secret Glasses Stealer? Jessica Finch did not even wear glasses. But maybe, just maybe, she stole some so she could look *even cleverer.*

Rare! A mini-mystery, on a school day, right here in Class 3T: the Mystery of the Teacher's Missing Glasses.

She, Judy Drewdy, was on the case.

During morning break, Judy stayed inside so she could investigate. She took out her torch and magnifying glass and searched on desks and under chairs. She searched in cubbies and in plastic tubbies. She searched behind the computer and the fish tank and the class guinea-pig cages.

All Detective Judy found were a sheet of wizard stickers (Rocky's), a glue stick (Frank's) and a pink pig paper clip that could only belong to one person – Jessica Finch, Pig Lover. Judy put the stickers in Rocky's folder, the glue stick in Frank's desk and the piggy paper clip on—

Wait just a Nancy Drew minute! Eagle Eye Moody spotted a clue on Jessica Finch's desk. Right on top of the spelling home-work was Jessica's pink piggy lunch box. Peeking out from an unzipped corner was what looked like one stolen pair of grown-up teacher glasses.

Judy unzipped the lunch box the rest

of the way. She got out her magnifying glass and turned on her torch.

Well, lookee here. Scoo-bee-doo! Mr Todd's missing glasses!

She, Judy Drewdy, had solved the crime, just like Nancy Drew. She would save the day *and* give the gift of sight back to Mr Todd.

Just then, Jessica Finch came back into the classroom. "Hey! What are you doing with my lunch box?" she asked.

"Nothing," said Judy, hiding the glasses behind her back.

"Mr Todd!" Jessica tattled. "I think Judy Moody is stealing my lunch. She's trying to take my pink chocolate cupcake!"

All eyes were on Judy Moody, Lunch Stealer, as the other third-graders filed back in. Fudge-a-roni! "I'm not the stealer. You are," said Judy.

"Oh, yeah? Then let's see what's behind your back."

"Girls? What seems to be the problem?" Mr Todd asked. "Judy, do you have something you'd like to show us?"

Judy Moody brought her hands out from behind her back. They were not holding a pink chocolate cupcake. They were holding ... Mr Todd's glasses.

"Uh!" the whole class gasped.

"*I* didn't steal them! Honest!" said Judy. "I found them in Jessica Finch's lunch box. *She* stole them. And I know why – so you wouldn't be able to *see* that she didn't finish writing her spelling words five times."

"I did, too!" Jessica flipped her paper over to show the words on the back.

"Nobody stole anything," said Mr Todd. "Jessica was showing me all the clever compartments inside her new lunch box this morning. I must have taken off my glasses to get a closer look."

"And they ended up inside my lunch box!" said Jessica.

"Judy, you know better than to go through someone else's personal things."

"But I was on a case! And I did find your glasses."

"That's no excuse. You wouldn't like Jessica going through your lunch box, would you? You need to apologize."

"Sorry," Judy mumbled.

She, Judy Moody, was in a mood. A why-do-I-always-get-in-trouble mood.

"OK, show's over. Take your seats. Mystery solved." Mr Todd put his glasses back on. "Except for the mystery of why I can't see through my glasses."

Jessica Finch pointed and laughed.

"Pink icing! From my cupcake."

Mr Todd wiped off the icing and licked his finger. He raised his eyebrows. He rubbed his glasses with a hankie. "Good as new," he said.

The Search for the Buried Backpack

Judy Moody, Frank and Rocky sat in the second-to-front row, waiting for the all-school assembly to start.

"Why did you bring your backpack?" asked Frank.

"It's not my backpack. It's my detective kit," Judy told her friends. "You never know when a mystery might pop up, just needing to be solved."

"In the main hall?" asked Rocky.

Judy frowned.

"I can't wait to meet Officer Mr Chips," said Frank.

"That's a funny name," said Judy.

"Not if you're a dog," Frank said, laughing.

"A police dog is coming here? To school?" Judy asked.

"Earth to Judy. Come in, Judy. Didn't you listen to anything Mr Todd told us this morning?" Rocky asked.

"Sorry," said Judy. "I was on a case."

"It's a police puppy," said Frank.

"Girls and boys," the head teacher announced, "as you know, October is Crime Prevention Month. We are very pleased to have with us today two crime fighters: Officer Kopp and his partner, Mr Chips."

A policeman in a dark blue uniform with patches on his sleeves came onstage. He was leading a brown puppy on a lead. The puppy had blue eyes, floppy ears and a shiny, wet nose. He was all legs, with huge puppy paws.

"Aw! So cute!" kids from the audience said all at once.

"I'm Officer Kopp, and this is Mr Chips," said the policeman. "Mr Chips is a chocolate Labrador. Labs are smart, friendly, dependable and good-natured. He likes to run, fetch and play ball. And he really likes kids."

Officer Kopp showed the kids how Mr Chips could chase after a ball and bring it back. Next, Mr Chips carried an egg in his mouth all the way across the stage without breaking it! The crowd went wild.

"Mr Chips is my best friend and my partner and the newest member of our K-9 team at the police department." Officer Kopp scratched the dog's head and patted him on the back.

"This little guy is learning to be a police dog. He's being trained to help us sniff out bad guys, search buildings and even locate stuff that's been stolen. This guy's sense of smell is so great that one day, Mr Chips might help us catch a bank robber or he could find a missing child."

"Mr Chips lives near my house,"
Jessica Finch bragged. "He wore a fancy
collar in the Fourth of July parade, and
I got to feed him dog treats!" It didn't
take a super-sleuth to figure out that
Jessica Finch was Miss Know-It-All.

The audience clapped like crazy for
Mr Chips.

"Does he eat bones?" a first-grader
asked.

"Mr Chips eats mostly puppy food.
And he likes doggie treats."

"Does he live at the police station?"
a fourth-grader asked.

"Nope. I'm his handler, so he lives at
home with me and my family."

"On my street!" Jessica Finch blurted.

Officer Kopp called on Stink. "Does he ride in your police car?" Stink asked.

"Mr Chips likes riding in cars more than anything. Every morning, he barks at me, begging to go for a ride. It's like he's saying, 'Car! Car! Car! Car! Car!'"

Officer Kopp stroked Mr Chips's ears. "Who's a car dog? You are. Oh yes, you are." Mr Chips gave Officer Kopp a giant slurp with his cherry-pink tongue.

The audience laughed. "And now I need some help from the audience," said Officer Kopp. "Anybody have an object they can bring up onstage? How about you, the young lady with the backpack?"

"Who? Me?" Judy asked, jumping up with a big smile.

"Yes. Bring your backpack up here, and let's give Mr Chips a whiff. Since he's at school today, we'll give him a test. A super-sniffing IQ test."

Judy climbed the steps to the stage. "This is my detective kit," she told Officer Kopp. "For solving mysteries."

"I like a person who's prepared for anything," said Officer Kopp, smiling. "Let's see if Mr Chips can solve a mystery, too. C'mon over and pet him. Then we'll let him sniff your backpack to pick up the scent."

Mr Chips sniffed Judy from head to toe, then he licked Judy's face all over with his pink slobbery tongue. *Slurp, slurp.*

"I hope you don't mind dog kisses," said Officer Kopp.

"Nope," said Judy. "They tickle!"

Next, Mr Chips sniffed Judy's backpack all over. Finally, Officer Kopp held the backpack up to Mr Chips's nose and gave him a voice command. "Find."

"OK, I'll take Mr Chips backstage now. That will give you a chance to hide your backpack. It's like a game of hide-and-seek. Ready?"

"Ready," said Judy.

Officer Kopp took Mr Chips behind the thick velvet curtain. "No peeking, Mr Chips!" Judy called over her shoulder.

Judy walked down the centre aisle, snaking through the first-graders. She cut through the row in front of the second-graders and hopped right over Stink's legs. Then she walked backwards all the way to the centre aisle.

"Hide it under Mr Todd's chair," yelled some third-graders. But Judy only walked around Mr Todd's chair, then zigzagged through the fourth- and fifth-graders.

"Behind the stands!" kids yelled.

"Hide it in the basketball hoop!"

"Rubbish bin! Rubbish bin!"

Finally, she stopped in front of the cupboard where the PE teacher kept all the gym balls, skipping ropes and orange cones. Judy checked to make sure Mr Chips wasn't watching. Quietly, she opened the door.

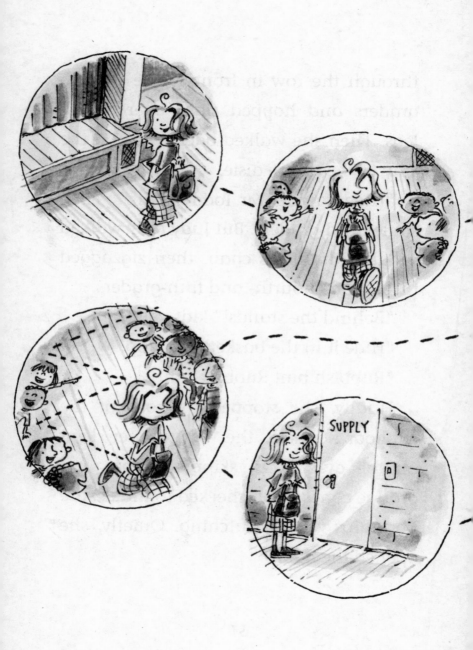

"Ooh-ee!" The cupboard was dusty and smelled like feet – Stink's smelly trainers times ten. Judy pinched her nose. "This smells so bad it's giving me a nose wedgie."

The audience laughed like crazy.

In the cupboard sat a big wire basket loaded with footballs and basketballs, volleyballs and kickballs. Judy buried her backpack deep down in the middle of the pile of dusty, dirty balls. Judy shut the door silently behind her and returned to the stage.

Everybody hushed when Mr Chips came out from behind the curtain. The puppy led Officer Kopp down the side steps. Then he padded down the centre aisle, following Judy's trail. He sniffed his way through the second grade, trotting up to Stink. He hopped over Stink's legs and sped up the centre aisle.

When he got to Mr Todd's chair, he ran in circles like crazy.

"He's chasing his tail!" yelled Frank.

"Give him a chance," somebody else yelled.

"C'mon, Mr Chips," Judy coaxed. "You can do it."

But Mr Chips had stopped in his tracks. He looked confused.

"Give him a minute," said Officer Kopp. "It's not over yet."

Suddenly, Mr Chips raised his nose in the air. He sniffed left. He sniffed right.

Zoom! He shot off again, zigzagging his way through the fourth- and fifth-graders. At last, he came to the door of the cupboard.

"*Arf! Arf! Arf-arf-arf,*" Mr Chips barked at the door. Officer Kopp opened the door. Mr Chips bounded in and knocked over the wire basket full of balls. *Boing! Boing!* Mr Chips pawed his way through the bouncing balls. In no time, he was trotting up to Officer Kopp, Judy's backpack hanging from his mouth.

The whole audience went cuckoo, clapping and cheering. "Good boy!" said Officer Kopp.

Mr Chips wagged his tail like crazy.

"Whoa." The crowd buzzed.

"How'd he do that?"

"Wow."

"It's magic."

Officer Kopp went back onstage with Mr Chips and took a bow. "Sergeant Super-Sniffer! The best partner a guy could have. Thanks, Virginia Dare School. You've been a great audience!"

Mr Chips hung out his tongue and wagged his windscreen-wiper tail. From where Judy sat, it almost looked as if Mr Chips was smiling.

The Mystery of the Missing Mr Chips

The next day, and the day after that, all anybody could talk about at Virginia Dare School was Sergeant Super-Sniffer, aka Mr Chips.

Then, late Friday afternoon, something happened. Something big. Judy was smack-dab in the middle of an important case – Nancy Drew book No.15: *The Haunted Bridge*, that is – when the loudspeaker crackled. Judy jumped two metres and yelled "Yurp," wrecking the *silent* in silent reading.

"Teachers and students," said the head teacher over the intercom. "I have an important announcement to make. Officer Kopp called to alert us that Mr Chips has gone missing!" This was terrible news. Awful news. No-good, way-bad news. "The dog was last seen in the Bird Neck neighbourhood on Abigail Lane at seven this morning."

"That's close to where I live," said Judy.

"That's *my street*," said Jessica Finch, pointing at herself.

"Since we all met Mr Chips just a few days ago and know what he looks like, Officer Kopp is asking us to please be on the lookout. If any of you super-sleuths out there spot Mr Chips, call 1-800-MR-CHIPS right away. Thank you."

Mr Chips was missing! Escaped! Lost! This was just about probably the worst announcement in the history of announcements at Virginia Dare School.

Wait just a Nancy Drew minute. She, Judy Moody, was smack-dab in the middle of a real-life, not-book mystery! A missing-persons case. A missing-*puppy* case, that is. For sure and absolute positive! In fact, this was almost like the time in *Nancy Drew: Girl Detective*, graphic novel No.6, when a chimp named Mr Cheeters, who was wearing a diamond necklace, went missing.

Maybe Mr Chips didn't escape or get lost. Maybe, just maybe, Mr Chips was *stolen*! As in kidnapped. As in *dog*napped. Maybe, just maybe, Mr Chips had been wearing a fancy-schmancy diamond doggy collar and some bad guy with an eye patch or a tattoo or a snaggle tooth had wanted it!

While Judy hoped nothing bad had happened to Mr Chips, she couldn't help wishing for a mystery. A real-life Nancy Drew mystery. This was a case for Judy Moody, Girl Detective. Judy Drewdy!

WWNDD? What Would Nancy Drew Do? She would take a deep breath and use her detective thinking, that's what. Judy wrote a note to all three members of the Toad Pee Club – Rocky, Frank and Stink.

WHO: Toad Pee Club Members
WHAT: Emergency Meeting
WHERE: Judy Moody Detective Agency
AKA TOAD PEE CLUB TENT
WHEN: After School
WHY: Big important mystery to solve
BE THERE OR BE A TOAD!

When they got to the Toad Pee Clubhouse after school, it wasn't the Toad
Pee Clubhouse any more. It was the JUDY
MOODY DETECTIVE AGENCY. That's what the
crooked sign duck-taped to the front tent
flap said. Inside were a chair, a lamp and
a poster that said WANTED: STUMPY, SNIGGS
AND SNORKY.

"I brought binoculars," said Rocky.

"I brought snoopware," said Frank. "You know, spy stuff. Telescope, sunglasses, fake noses and walkie-talkies."

"I brought ... my ... super-sniffer nose. For sniffing out clues," said Stink. "So what's the big mystery?"

"I think Mr Chips was stolen," said Judy. "Fact: Jessica Finch lives across the street from Mr Chips, and she told me at lunch that no way would he ever run away from Officer Kopp. Fact: Jessica Finch said that Mr Chips has a fancy collar. He wore it in the Fourth of July parade. Fact: Bad-guy burglars could have taken him to get their hands on his diamond doggy collar."

"Jessica Finch doesn't know every-thing," said Stink.

"Ya-huh. Why do you think we call her Miss Know-It-All?" said Frank.

"We should start at Officer Kopp's house. Scene of the crime," said Judy. "But wait! First I have to swear you in."

"I'm not allowed to use swear words," said Stink.

"Stink, in Detective Land, that means you take a super-serious oath and promise to be a good assistant detective and help solve the mystery."

Judy handed a name-tag sticker to each boy. "Here, wear these on your shirts. Agent Stink. Agent Pearl. Agent Rock."

"I want to be Agent 714," said Stink.

"And can I be Agent Dragnet?" asked Frank.

"How come mine says *Agent Rock,* not *Rocky*?" asked Rocky.

"It sounds cooler," said Judy. She took out a set of dino-bug pins.

"Hey, those are my paleo-insect pins!" said Stink.

"Why do we have to wear these?" asked Agent Rock.

"Quit *bugging* me," said Judy, passing out the pins. "All detectives wear badges. These are your official badges."

"Can I be the stinkbug?" asked Stink.

Judy handed Stink a yucky millipede.

"I said Agent Dragnet, not Agent Dragonfly," said Frank.

Rocky/Agent Rock pinned on the Jurassic beetle.

"Fine," said Judy. "I'll be the cockroach."

"I know how we can make real badges," said Stink. "I saw it on television. First you take cardboard and cut out the shape of a shield. Then you glue silver foil—"

"Stink. This is no time for arts-and-crafts class."

"Fine," said Stink. "I'll be the ladybird. But I'm going to pretend it's a prehistoric stinkbug, and you can't stop me."

"Raise your right hands and repeat after me," said Judy. "I, Agent Stink, Pearl or Rock..."

"I, Agent Stink, Pearl or Rock..."

"Do solemnly swear..."

"Do solemnly swear..."

"Even though I'm not allowed to swear," said Stink.

"That I will obey all detective laws..."

"That I will obey all detective laws..."

"And listen to Judy..."

"And listen to Judy..."

"Because she is the WBMS – World's Best Mystery Solver…"

"Because she is the—"

"You said *BM*," said Stink. "You can't make me say *BM*."

Judy grinned. "Never mind." She put on her own cockroach badge and pointed down the street. "To the crime scene!"

Before you could say *Password to Larkspur Lane,* Judy and her two assistants (plus one stinky brother) were *knock-knock*ing on Officer Kopp's front door.

"I'll do the talking," said Judy, elbowing her way to the front. Officer Kopp came to the door in his blue jeans and sock feet. He was holding his phone in one hand and a stack of flyers in the other.

Judy started her speech. "Hi, we're from Virginia Dare School—"

"These aren't bug pins," Stink interrupted. "They're badges."

Judy turned on Stink and gave him her best Hercules-beetle stare. "We heard about

Mr Chips and we're detectives and—"

"Detectives, huh?" said Officer Kopp.

"Where's your uniform?" Frank asked, staring at Officer Kopp's socks.

"We rushed right over as soon as we heard that Mr Chips had been stolen," Rocky added.

"We don't know that he's been stolen," said Officer Kopp. "Most likely he just escaped, though for the life of me, I can't see how. But I sure am glad to see you guys."

Judy stood up straighter. "You are?"

"Sure. I was hoping you kids might help put up flyers around town." He held up flyers that said LOST in big letters and showed a cute picture of Mr Chips.

"We'll put them up at Fur and Fangs," said Rocky.

"And Speedy Market," said Frank.

"And all over the whole entire town," said Stink.

"Great!" said Officer Kopp.

Judy took out her notebook. "So Mr Chips was last seen where?"

"In the back garden this morning," said Officer Kopp.

"Uh-huh," said Judy. Scribble, scribble. "When was this?"

"My wife let him out at around six thirty, I think. Then I filled his dish and put him in the kennel around seven. At seven forty-five, I went out to get him, and he was gone. And the food was still in his dish."

"Uh-huh, uh-huh," said Judy. Scribble.

"Poor Mr Chips," said Frank.

"Can we see the kennel?" Judy asked. A good detective always took a look at the scene of the crime.

"Sure. Come around to the back," said Officer Kopp. In his sock feet, he led them back to a tidy, fenced-in back garden. Along the side was a kennel, much bigger than a doghouse, made out of chain-link fencing.

Officer Kopp scratched the back of his head. "He's never done anything like this before. The whole garden's fenced, and the kennel is supposed to be escape-proof."

The kennel door was latched with a U-shaped hook. "Was the latch open when you came out at seven forty-five?" Judy asked.

"That's just it. The latch was still closed, and the door wasn't open."

Scribble. "Have you seen any suspicious characters lurking around?"

"Anybody with a name like Grumpy or Scurvy?" Stink asked.

"Not that I know of. This is a quiet neighbourhood." Just then the phone rang from inside. "They're patching calls through, and the phone's been ringing off the wall. Maybe it's a lead. 'Scuse me." Officer Kopp trotted towards the house.

Judy tapped her pencil on her pad. "Fact: door is closed, latch down. Fact: dog food still in dish. If you were going to run away, wouldn't you finish your breakfast first?"

The boys nodded.

"Brilliant idea number sixty-seven," said Judy. "Get in the cage, Stink. We'll latch the door and see if you can break out."

"Is this a trick? Are you going to lock me in the kennel and run away?"

"This is not a trick. It's a real detective thing to act stuff out so you can figure out what happened. C'mon, Stinker, you took the oath."

Stink dragged his feet into the kennel,

and Judy flipped the latch down. "Now act like a dog."

"I'm not gonna crawl around on all fours and pretend I'm a dog!"

"Dogs can't talk, Stink."

"Arf!" Stink got down on all fours and pawed at the air.

"Now bump up against the door of the kennel. Don't use your hands."

Stink bumped against the chain-link door. "Ow!" He rubbed his shoulder.

"See?" said Judy. "He can't open it. And he's much bigger than Mr Chips." She bent to the ground, looking for more clues with her pocket magnifying glass.

"Aha!" she shrieked so loudly that all three boys jumped.

"Did you see a bad guy?"

"Did you see a burglar?"

"Did you see a bear?"

"No, but I saw bad-guy-burglar boot prints the size of a bear. Look." She pointed to a patch of mud in front of the kennel door.

"They're probably just Officer Kopp's footprints," said Rocky.

"Or a bad guy like Stumpy or Snorky," said Judy.

"But they're *gi*-normous," said Stink. "As big as four footprints put together. Give me your ruler so I can measure them."

"I don't have a ruler," said Judy.

"That whole detective kit and no ruler?"

"In *The Witch Tree Symbol*, Nancy Drew used her skirt as a ruler."

"Then give me your skirt."

"Hardee-har-har, Stink."

"No way are these footprints human," said Frank.

"Maybe Mr Chips got eaten by a bear!" said Rocky.

"Or a yeti!" said Stink.

"The Abominable Snowman," said Frank.

"Get real," said Judy.

"There are more footprints over here," said Stink. "These look more like trainers."

"Stink, get a clue. Those are your prints," said Judy.

Frank pointed at something caught on the fence. "Judy. Over here!"

"What have we here?" Judy asked. "A clump of fur!"

"Could be from the dog," said Agent Rock.

"Or a yeti," said Agent Pearl.

"Move over. Let the Nose take a whiff." Stink sniffed it and turned up his nose. "It's dog hair, all right. P.U.! Smells worse than a yeti."

"When's the last time you smelled a yeti?" Judy took out her tweezers and collected the dog-hair evidence in a plastic zip-top bag.

"So do you think Mr Chips brushed up against the fence when he was being dragged out by bad guys?" Frank asked.

"Dognappers!" Judy whispered.

"You think somebody *stole* Mr Chips? For real?" asked Rocky.

"Hello! Read the clues," said Detective Judy. "One, Mr Chips didn't even get to finish his breakfast. Two, he can't open the latch on the door himself. And three, bad-guy big-foot boot prints are everywhere."

"Burglars!" said Rocky.

"Thieves!" said Frank.

"Dog stealers!" said Stink.

She, Eagle-Eye-Moody, had found one clue after another, just like Nancy Drew. She had read the evidence. She was on her way to cracking the big case. All she had to do now was track down a couple of downright dirty dognappers with size sixteen stompers!

The Case of
the Dog-Bone Bandit

The next morning, Judy was already hard at work on the case by the time Stink woke up. She was sprawled on the floor with a rainbow of marker pens all around her.

"What're you doing to Officer Kopp's flyers?" Stink asked.

"Fixing them," said Judy, colouring in blue eyes on the picture of Mr Chips.

Stink tilted his head, reading upside

down. He was trying to figure out the words Judy had just added. "'Have you seen this goo?'"

"'Have you seen this *dog*.'"

"Oh. Your *D* looks like an *O*."

"Stink, a good detective can read backwards and upside down." Judy coloured in a black letter *R*.

"'*Drawer?*'" Stink asked, squinching up his face.

"'*Reward!*'" said Judy. "We have to offer big bucks so that anyone who has seen Mr Chips or has any information on his whereabouts will call the police. Rule Number One of being a good detective is don't be afraid to ask for help."

"You mean Rule Number *One Gazillion*!" said Stink. "So, whoever finds Mr Chips gets a reward, not a drawer?"

"Yep."

"So if I find him," Stink asked, "I get the money?"

Judy ignored him. She wrote $23.80.

"Whoa," said Stink. "Twenty-three dollars and eighty cents. That's a lot of money. How'd you come up with $23.80?"

"That's all you had in your piggy bank, Stink."

"You broke my bank?" Stink ran into his room and grabbed his piggy bank. "That's weird. My bank's not broken... And the lock is still on," he said. He put the piggy bank up to his ear and shook it. Empty.

"The Mystery of the Missing Money," said Judy.

"You picked the lock! With one of those Nancy Drew kirby grip thingies."

"You can't prove it, Stink."

"No fair! You can't just keep taking my stuff. First it was my president dollars, then my dino-bug pins. Now this. That's called stealing. It makes you just as bad as Snarky, Snuffy and Stingy – those Nancy Drew bad guys."

"For your information, it's Snorky, Sniggs and Stumpy."

"Whatever. It's still my money."

"Well, you stole a whole bag of my

gummy mice. Just think, Stink. If you find Mr Chips, you can win back your money."

"But that money's already mine! I shouldn't have to win it back."

"It's for a good cause," Judy reminded him. "If you ask me, that lock was just asking to be picked."

"Give it!" said Stink, holding out his hand.

"ROAR," said Judy, handing over the money. Now she had to think of something else to offer as a reward. Something good. Something anybody would want a whole big bunch. She looked around her room at her collections. At last she had an idea.

LOST! HAVE YOU SEEN THIS DOG?

IF FOUND:

Friendly Chocolate Lab.
BROWN & FURRY.
ANSWERS TO NAME "MR CHIPS"

LAST SEEN IN BIRD NECK NEIGHBOURHOOD

REWARD

7 Pizza Tables   3 Grouchy pencils
17 Gummymice Sweets
100 Plasters
1 MOOD Ring
1 MOON ROCK (if he lets me)

CALL
1·800·MRCHIPS

P.S.
To collect Reward come to 117 CReaker ROAD ASK FOR JUDY

❂ ❂ ❂

Before you could say *Sign of the Twisted Candles*, Judy and Stink, with tyres full of air, were speeding their way to Speedy

Market to put up flyers. Judy's old turquoise bike wasn't *exactly* a Nancy Drew blue roadster convertible. But the wind did whip her messy hair around, and the October sun warmed her cheeks.

Judy and Stink met Rocky and Frank outside the supermarket.

"We already hit Fur and Fangs and Screamin' Mimi's," said Frank.

"And the bakery, the bowling alley and the birthday party store," said Rocky.

"Rare!" said Judy.

Inside Speedy Market, tons of people and a reporter and lights and cameras were crowded around, and the store manager was talking to a cop. Not just any cop. *Officer* Kopp!

"I'm not kidding you," Mr Keene, the manager, told Officer Kopp. "That little guy headed straight for the pet food aisle like nobody's business. Crazy pup grabbed a bone worth $2.79. I yelled, 'Drop it!' Did he drop it? No, sirree. He ran straight out of the front door before anybody could catch him."

"Sorry about the bone, Mike," said Officer Kopp. "I'll pay you back."

"That's one smart pup. How he knew which aisle had the dog treats..."

"Is that all the suspect seems to have taken?" asked a lady reporter.

"Suspect? He's a dog, for crying out loud," said Mr Keene.

"Did you get a look at the shoplifter?"

"Yeah," said Mr Keene. "Brown and hairy." He turned to Officer Kopp. "I guess you could say instead of taking a bite *out of* crime, he took a bite *into* crime."

The reporter turned to the camera and spoke into her puffy microphone. "A thief remains at large after a daring heist in the pet food aisle of the local Speedy Market," she said. "You might say the four-legged man's best friend was too *speedy* for this market manager." She fake-smiled at the camera. "Cut!"

Judy followed Officer Kopp out of the store. "Do they think it was Mr Chips?" she asked.

"All anybody saw was a streak of brown and a tail, but it must have been him. Keep looking!" Officer Kopp called as he hopped into his police car and headed out of the car park, lights flashing.

Judy and her best chums (the Nancy Drew word for friends) searched all over the car park of Speedy Market – under cars, behind a tree, in the bins. They asked every shopper they saw, "Did you happen to see a little brown puppy with big paws?" But the answer was always no. Until ... a lady with funny glasses pointed to the back corner of the car park. "Those men in that van had a dog."

"Where? What van?" asked Judy, snapping her head around.

"Was he brown?"

"Was he cute?"

"Was he Mr Chips?"

Just then, a dark green van peeled out, tearing through the car park, tyres squealing. Judy and her friends jumped out of the way. The van swerved out of the car park without stopping.

"Stop! Thief!" Judy yelled, but the van sped off down the street before she could make out the letters on the number plate.

"Did you see that? It has to be them – the bad-guy dognappers!" Judy was breathing fast and pointing down the street. "This is SO just like Nancy Drew mystery No.1: *The Secret of the Old Clock*."

"How is this like some old clock?" Rocky asked.

"C'mon, guys. You read the book."

"No, we didn't," all three boys said at the same time.

"First of all, there's a dark van. Second of all, there's this girl named Judy. She's trying to cross the street and she almost gets hit by a moving van and she falls off a bridge and Nancy Drew has to rescue her and it turns out the bad-guy jewel thieves stole an old clock and stuff."

"I thought you said the jewel thieves were in *The Mystery of the Brass Bound Trunk*," said Stink.

"And *The Mystery at Lilac Inn* and *The Ghost of Blackwood Hall* and—"

"Wow, Nancy Drew must have more jewels than the Queen of England!"

"She doesn't get to keep them, Stink." Judy took out her notebook. "So, did anybody see anything? Like a number plate?"

"The first three letters were K-G-B," said Rocky.

"K-F-C," said Frank.

"K-L-F," said Stink. "Or E-L-F."

"Great," said Judy, putting her pencil behind her ear. "So we know who took Mr Chips. Some secret bad guys who eat chicken and look like elves."

"I think one guy did have pointy ears," said Stink.

"*ROAR*," said Judy. "What about the van? Did it say anything on it?"

"Flush 'n' Flo?" said Stink.

"Push and Go," said Rocky.

"Flash and Glo," said Frank.

"Toilet emergency!" said Stink.

"Stink, not now."

"It had the words *Toilet Emergency* on the side. I saw. For real. No lie."

"Stink's right," said Frank.

Judy chewed on the end of her pencil. "Toilet emergency. Flush 'n' Flo. So they must be like those guys that fix toilets and stuff. RARE!"

"The super-bad guys are plumbers?" Frank asked.

"That's just their cover," Judy explained. "Everybody knows that international jewel thieves can't ride around in a van that says *Jewel Thieves*."

"The phone number was like 1-800-UN-DOG," said Rocky.

"'UN-DOG?'" said Judy. "Are you sure it didn't say 'UN-*CLOG*?'"

"1-800-UNDER-DOG!" said Stink.

"Great," said Judy. "Let's all take an

Underdog Super Energy Pill and find a phone box and change into super-heroes. Then we'll find Mr Chips."

"Hip, hip, hip and away we go!" yelled Stink.

"I know," said Frank. "Let's stake out the supermarket till they come back."

"Yeah, we know Mr Chips is hungry, right?"

"Yeah, 'cos why else would a cop dog steal a dog bone?" Frank said.

"I can't believe Mr Chips is a shop-lifter," said Rocky.

"I don't think Mr Chips is the thief," said Judy. "I bet these guys are so bad, they're not even feeding him, so poor Mr Chips has to steal his own food!"

"He's still gonna have to arrest himself for breaking the law." Frank cracked himself up. Rocky and Stink cracked up, too.

"This isn't helping us find Mr Chips," said Judy.

"Rule Number One," said Stink. "A good detective always keeps a sense of humour."

The Case of the Troublesome Toilet

The rest of Saturday, and all day Sunday, Judy and her fellow junior detectives biked all over the neighbourhood in search of a dark green van. They saw black vans, blue vans, brown vans, maroon vans, but not one single green van with *Toilet Emergency* written on its side and driven by chicken-eating guys with pointy ears.

On Monday morning, she, Judy

Moody, was in a mood. A why-can't-I-solve-a-mystery mood. Then came a clue, when she least expected it.

Judy was doodling paw prints with her Grouchy pencil through Mr Todd's talk about Healthy Habits when out of the blue, the head teacher came on the loudspeaker and said three magic words.

"Girls and boys, I'm afraid we have a bit of *toilet* trouble in the third-fourth wing. We had an *emergency* this morning when a pipe burst and flooded the girls' bathroom. The *plumbers* are here to fix the problem, but we ask that you use the bathrooms by the library until further notice."

Toilet! Emergency! Plumbers! Those three words were music to Judy's ears.

She craned her neck to look out into the car park. That's when she saw it: a dark green van, parked right across from the entrance to the school!

Judy took out her notebook and wrote *SOS* in red lipstick. She held it up for Frank and Rocky to see. Her hand shot up. "Mr Todd, I have to go. Badly. And Rocky and Frank have to go, too." The whole class cracked up. Frank turned beetroot-red. "To the bathroom, I mean."

Jessica Finch raised her hand. "Mayday! Mayday! I have to go, too." Jessica Finch was just being a big fat copycat. What a Fink-Face.

"Tell you what," said Mr Todd. "Let's all take a quick toilet break."

Eagle-Eye Moody was back on the case.

Judy, Rocky and Frank rushed out the door and down the hall. They did not head for the bathroom by the library. They headed straight for the girls' room with the busted toilet. On their way, they ran smack-dab into Agent Stink.

"Stink, the girls' bathroom is broken and the bad-guy plumbers are here fixing it. No lie!" Judy told him.

"Judy saw the van parked outside," said Frank. "It's green, just like the one at Speedy Market."

"Mr Chips could be right here right now!" said Rocky.

"This is big, Stink. And we only have

five minutes. Be our lookout while we check out the bathroom."

"What? You can't go in there. There might be exploding toilets! Or bad guys! They could tie you up. Or give you a major flushie or something."

"A flushie?" asked Judy.

"That's when they stick your head in the toilet ... and flush!" Frank whispered.

"Rule Number One, Stink: don't be afraid of flushies." Judy reached in her pocket and pulled out her SOS lipstick. "If anything happens, I'll write *SOS* on the mirror. Besides, I've got backup. Agent Rock and Agent Pearl are going in with me."

"I'm not going in the girls' room,"

Rocky and Frank said at the same time.

"We've got to," said Judy. "For Mr Chips!"

"Hurry up," said Stink, glancing up and down the hall. "Just yell 'Toilet paper' if you get into trouble."

Judy ducked under the yellow DO NOT CROSS tape. Her heart was beating in her throat as she tiptoed inside. Rocky and Frank followed close behind.

"Hey, it's pink!" Rocky whispered.

"And *the girls* have *soap*," said Frank.

"Shh!" said Judy. The place was quiet. Too quiet. A door from one of the stalls leaned against the sink. "Who's there?" she asked, holding her breath. She held out her Grouchy pencil for protection.

She inched closer to the far end of the bathroom and poked her head around the corner of the last stall.

"AAAGH!" screamed Judy. Rocky and Frank jumped back.

"What! Nobody's in here," said Rocky.

"I know. But I had a scream in me, all ready to come out."

"Toilet paper! Toilet paper!" Stink yelled, rushing into the girls' room.

"False alarm, Stink," said Frank. "They're not even here."

"No, but they *were* here," said Judy, pointing to tools left on the floor.

"Maybe they flushed themselves down the toilet!" said Stink.

"Stink, you have flushies on the brain."

that game, Cluedo."

the pipe, in the pipe

they're phantom plumbers,"

said Stink. "Like that phantom horse in Nancy Drew No.5: *The Secret of Shadow Ranch*."

Judy blinked. "Nice work, Agent Stinkbug. How'd you know that?"

"Um, you told me." Judy shook her head. "I, um, might have seen it on Sophie of the Elves's desk, and I might have just happened to take a peek."

"Phantom or not, they were here," said Rocky. "And where there are fake plumbers with a green van, Mr Chips can't be far behind."

...can feel

it," said Judy. "I'd bet my mood ring they keep Mr Chips tied up with this rope while they fake like they're fixing toilets."

"But where are they now?" Rocky asked.

Judy twisted the SOS lipstick,

"Poor Mr Chi...

"We're getting w...

doggy, all r...

Stink...

fraye...

Frank picked up a piece of old...

"The plumber did it, with th...

pink room. It's like a...

"Maybe...

said...

her detective brain spinning round and round. "I've got it." She snapped her fingers. "They left in a big fat hurry because they know we know."

"How do you know they know we know?" asked Frank.

"I don't know. Call it a Nancy Drew hunch. I just know they know we know."

"I know my head hurts," said Stink.

"We'd better hurry up and get out of here," said Frank.

"Before Fink-Face tattles on us," said Judy.

"It's early dismissal today," said Rocky, checking his watch. "Only twelve minutes before school's out."

"Hey, you guys have soap in your

bathroom? Pink soap?" Stink asked.

"Since when is everyone I know such a clean freak?" Judy asked.

All four kids made a beeline for the door. They passed Ms Tuxedo in the hall. "Did you see which way the plumbers went?" Judy and her fellow detectives asked at the same time. "Did they have pointy ears? Did you hear a dog barking?"

"You kids had better get back to class," said Ms Tuxedo. "The bell's about to ring any minute now."

For the last twelve minutes of the school day, Judy Moody had ants in her pants. Bees in her knees. Bug eggs in her legs. Who could sit still when the green van might be back any minute?

Scoo-bee-doo, Nancy Drew! An international ring of thieves, right here at Virginia Dare School! With Judy Drewdy and her crack detectives on the case, those thieves' dognapping days were numbered.

At last the bell rang. Judy raced to the car park. Still no green van in sight. "All aboard," yelled the bus driver. Judy waited till the last possible second. Still no van. She hopped on the bus. The doors whooshed shut as the bus pulled out of the car park. Judy pressed her nose to the window of Bus 211.

There it was! A green van! A green van that said WE FIX TOILETS AND OTHER PLUMBING EMERGENCIES. A green van that said CALL 1-555-UNCLOG-U on the side.

That was it! It was them! Stink and Rocky saw it, too.

"STOP!" cried Judy. "Stop the bus!"

The bus driver could not stop for one kid with a not-toilet emergency. The bus driver would not stop for a solve-a-mystery emergency. The bus driver had a way-big important schedule to keep.

Judy took out her Nancy Drew lipstick and wrote *SOS* on the back window of the school bus.

The bus driver still would not let Judy off the bus. The bus driver told Judy to sit down. The bus driver did not know that in that van might be Mr Chips.

From the back of the bus, Judy watched the green van disappear until it was no bigger than a bug. The wheels on the bus went round and round. Judy's detective heart went *pound, pound, pound*. What if Mr Chips was never, ever, ever found?

"I'll find you, Mr Chips. Don't you worry," she whispered to nobody but herself and the universe.

to call a plumber. The bad guys in the green van will come right to our house. We'll flush 'em out and rescue Mr Chips! Get it?"

"Genius!" said Judy. Just then, Stink flushed the toilet. *Spew!* Water sprayed up out of the toilet in a geyser and gushed all over the floor. Judy leaped out of the way. Mouse sprang on to the rim of the bath.

"Toilet emergency! Toilet emergency!" Stink yelled.

Mum and Dad came running up the stairs. "Judy," said Mum, "if this is another one of your Boston Tub Parties—"

"Stink did it!" said Judy, pointing at her brother.

"Mouse did it!" said Stink, pointing at the cat.

"Out of the way, Stink, so I can turn off the water," said Dad, reaching behind the toilet.

"We have to call a plumber!" said Stink.

Judy tried to help. "We should call those guys Flush and Flo, or Push and Go, or Flash and Glo. The guys in the green van."

Mum put on rubber gloves. She pulled Darth Vader out of the toilet. "We're not calling a plumber. Plumbers are very expensive."

Dad plunged the toilet until the water went down.

"I don't know what you two were up to," said Dad, "but you kids are going to clean up this mess."

Mum handed her rubber gloves to Judy.

"Grab a bucket, Suds," said Judy. "I'll get the mop, and we'll clean up the scene of the crime." So much for the Judy Moody Detective Agency. It was more like the Mop and Bucket Brigade.

@   @   @

As soon as the bathroom was sparkling clean, Judy and Stink ran outside to meet Rocky and Frank at the old manhole. "Somebody in this neighbourhood has got to have a broken toilet for real," said Stink.

"Let's knock on doors and ask," said Judy. "But if anybody wants your name, use a fake one, just in case. In *The Thirteenth Pearl*, Nancy Drew uses the alias Nan Drewry."

"I'll be James Madison. Judy, you be Elizabeth Blackwell."

"Duh. Everybody knows we're not them," said Judy.

"OK, then I'll be James Madagascar," said Stink.

"I'll be Liz Inkwell."

"Spuds Houdini," said Rocky.

"Dills Pickle," said Frank.

Liz Inkwell rang bells. Dills Pickle knocked on doors. They asked, "Is your toilet broken?" But not one single house in the whole entire state of Virginia, it seemed, had a broken toilet. Not even a stopped-up sink or a semi-flooded basement.

"We'll never find Mr Chips," said Liz Inkwell. "Nancy Drew would have found him three days ago. First, she would have been kidnapped, bound and gagged, and thrown in a river. But by now she'd be at the River Heights Police Station collecting a big, fat medal."

"Boo-hoo, Nancy Drew," said James Madagascar. "Rule Number One: a good detective does not get in a bad mood."

"You're right, Stink. A good detective always keeps her spirits up."

Judy shook herself to shake off her

bad mood. "Eureka! I've got it! If those thieves know we're on to them, maybe they're not pretending to be plumbers any more."

"A dognapper could pretend to look like anybody," said Rocky.

"Yeah, an old lady. A dog walker. An elf. A clown," said Judy.

"How about a postman?" asked Frank, pointing across the street.

"Hey, it's Jack Frost!" said Stink as they ran towards his post van. "Is your toilet broken, by any chance?"

"Have you seen a green van around here?" Frank asked.

"How about any cute, brown and hairy dogs?" Judy asked.

"Who answer to the name of Mr Chips?" asked Stink.

"Or any sneaky bad guys who look like plumbers?" Frank asked.

"Or any old ladies or clowns who look like sneaky bad guys?" Rocky asked.

"One question at a time! Let's see..." Jack Frost scratched his beard. "I did see Mildred Benson's Chihuahua. But he's not cute. And he's not hairy. I haven't seen any green vans, just two white cable TV trucks. No suspicious old ladies today. And not one single clown."

"Roar," said Judy.

"But there is one thing that's strange. Might be a mystery."

"What? What?" they all said at once.

"What is it? Tell us!"

Jack Frost held up an empty sandwich bag. "I packed a lunch this morning and put it in the van. But when I got back to the van at lunchtime after walking my route, my food was missing."

"Strange," said Stink.

"Weird," said Rocky and Frank.

"Interesting," said Judy. She peered closely at the plastic bag. She held it up to the light. "Was it a corned beef sandwich?"

"Yes. Yes, it was."

"Did your corned beef sandwich have mustard?"

"Yes. Yes, it did," said Jack Frost.

"How did you know that?" asked Rocky.

She pointed with her Grouchy pencil. "There's a mustard fingerprint right here. And I can smell the corned beef."

"So it was Colonel Mustard, with the corned beef sandwich, in the post van!"

"Or," said Stink, "maybe a koala ate the corned beef sandwich."

Judy shot him a super-sidewinder stare. A poison-dart-frog glare. "What?"

"Fact," said Stink. "Koalas are one of the only animals with fingerprints. And a koala's fingerprint looks almost exactly like a human's."

"I didn't see a single koala in the kitchen while I was making the sandwich, so I guess that mustard print is mine," said Jack Frost.

"So the fingerprint is just a red herring," Judy said.

"What's a red herring?" asked Stink.

"A P.U. stinky fish," said Rocky.

"No, a false clue," Judy told them. "To throw us off. That means... Hypers! The missing corned beef sandwich is the clue, not the mustard fingerprint. We're lucky we stumbled on it, just like Nancy Drew in *The Clue in the Crumbling Wall*."

"But how is the corned beef sandwich a clue if it's missing?"

"Don't you get it? The bad guys are training Mr Chips to steal stuff. You saw how smart he was at school that day. First it was my backpack. Then it was a dog bone; now it's people food. Think what could be next. Diamonds? Jewels? Or will they train him to rob a bank?"

"Oh no," said Frank. "Mr Chips is turning into a jewel thief."

"Or a bank robber," said Rocky.

"Or a clock stealer," said Stink. "Like in Judy's book."

"Sounds like your Mr Chips has gone over to the dark side," said Jack Frost, opening up the back of his post van. It was heaped with bags full of post.

"Yeah, we'll have to call him Mr Darth Vader Chips," said Frank.

Suddenly, she, Judy Moody, could not believe her eagle eyes! In the back of the post van, she spied a bunch of magazines tied up *with rope*. Rope exactly like the rope the plumbers had. Rope that could be used to tie up Mr Chips! *Jack Frost, fake postman, with the rope, in the post van!*

"Who is this Mr Chips, anyway?" asked Jack Frost. "Some kind of canine criminal?"

"Like you don't know," Judy muttered. Then, louder, "Where'd you get this rope? Do you like dogs? Did you really lose your corned beef sandwich? You say that was *your* fingerprint? Are all those post bags really for post?" *Pow. Pow. Pow.* Judy fired detective questions at her new suspect.

Stink yanked on her arm and pulled her to the other side of the street. "Are you cuckoo?" he whispered. "Why are you being such a meanie to Jack Frost?"

"Rule Number One, Stink: everyone's a suspect. Didn't you see that rope he had in the back of his post van? It's just like the rope used to tie up Mr Chips. Admit it, Stinker, Jack Frost could be working with the dognappers. He could be part of a ring of international jewel thieves!"

"Hel-*lo*! Jack Frost is not a thief," said Stink. "He's a postman. And he's my friend. Look at him – he looks like Santa Claus."

"That's just it," said Judy. "Anybody can be a bad guy. Even Santa Claus. Think about it, Stink. One – a postman always carries dog treats. He could be helping the bad guys train Mr Chips to sniff out the loot for stealing. Two – he knows when people go on holiday, so he could case the neighbourhood and tip off the bad guys when people aren't home. And three – what's the perfect place to hide loot like

 diamonds? A postbag. Pretty soon, nobody will get any post, and there won't be any jewels left in the whole state of Virginia. I rest my case."

"Jack Frost gave you mittens for Christmas! Jack Frost made it snow! Would a jewel thief give you mittens? Would a dognapper make it snow for

Christmas?" Stink ripped off his bug-pin badge and handed it to Judy. "I quit!" he huffed.

"Before you quit," said Judy, "go and ask Jack Frost where he got that rope."

Stink crossed his arms. He uncrossed his arms. He walked over to Jack Frost. Judy came along behind him. He asked about the magazines tied up with rope.

"Oh, I'm just helping out Mrs Stratemeyer down the street. She's old and can't get out, so she bundles up her used magazines and I recycle them for her."

"Aha! So you *did* see an old lady today," said Judy. *Liar, liar, pants on fire.*

"Sure," said Jack Frost. "Well, the post won't deliver itself." Jack Frost hopped back into the van and started it up. "Let me know if you find that sandwich!" he called.

"See?" said Stink. "The rope is just one of those stinky red fish."

"Red herring," said Rocky and Frank at the same time.

"Herring, schmerring. I rest *my* case," said Judy. Just then she realized that the post van had started off down the street. "Wait! What was that old lady's name? How do you spell it? And what street does she live on?"

But it was too late. Jack Frost's rear lights were already turning the corner.

The Case of the
Curious Cookie Crumbs

The next day, she, Judy Moody, was in a mood. An UN-detective mood. A bummed-out, not-Nancy-Drew mood. Not one clue so far had led to finding Mr Chips. Nancy Drew made it all look so easy-peasy even if she was in an avalanche or being strangled by a python. But what if Judy Moody, Girl Detective, never cracked the case? What if Mr Chips never made it home?

Mystery UNsolved. Judy wondered if Nancy Drew ever had an unsolved case. She didn't think so. Rule Number One: never give up!

Judy sat at the third-grade lunch table. In between bites of peanut-butter-and-banana sandwich, she made a list of suspects in her detective notebook:

Plumbers in green van

JACK FROST?

JESSICA FINCH (HA, HA— I WISH!)

Old Lady, begins with an S

The trail had gone cold. The green van had been at school again this morning, but it was gone by lunch. The toilet in the girls' bathroom was fixed. And Jack Frost was just delivering post, like he did every day. Even old Mrs S was probably just some nice old lady like Mrs Abby Rowen in Nancy Drew No.1: *The Secret of the Old Clock.* Some nice lady who liked to recycle.

Judy was miles away when she heard Jessica Finch bark from across the table, "Hey, my lunch! Somebody ... Judy Moody stole my lunch for real this time!"

"Me too!" said Matthew.

"Me three!" said Jordan. The whole third-grade lunch table stared at Judy with goggly eyes.

Judy popped up out of her chair and peered into Jessica's pink piggy lunch box. "Was it a corned beef sandwich?" she asked.

"Fail. Guess again," said Jessica.

"Did you have a corned beef sandwich?" Judy asked Matthew.

"Nope."

"Did you have a corned beef sandwich?" Judy asked Jordan.

Jordan shook her head *no*. "But somebody spilled my salad everywhere."

"Somebody smushed my hummus sandwich," said Matthew.

"And somebody spilled all the apples out of my Apple Curry Turkey Pita!" Jessica Finch squeaked.

"What are you guys? The Health-Nut Lunch Club or something?"

Jessica looked at Matthew and Jordan. "We're the Tofu Triplets." Jessica was so not kidding.

Judy laughed, and milk sprayed out her nose.

"We bring healthy stuff for our lunches and share. Today I brought an organic chocolate-chip cookie for everybody," said Jessica. "And now mine is G-O-N-E, gone! All that's left are a few lousy crumbs."

"That's the way the cookie crumbles," Judy teased.

"Mine's gone, too," said Matthew.

"Me three," said Jordan.

"And we know who stole them." All three of the Tofu Triplets pointed at Judy Moody. "Give us back our cookies, you crummy cookie crook!"

"Crumbs to that. Why would I steal a chocolate-chip cookie when I have my own right he—" She lifted up her sandwich. She searched under her napkin. "Aye-crumba! Somebody stole *my* cookie, too." Something strange was going on at Virginia Dare School. And getting stranger by the minute.

"Jessica, did you have your lunch box with you at all times today?"

"Some detective," said Jessica. "Mr Todd told us to drop our lunches out here before going to the library, remember?

Anybody could have got into them."

"I bet it was a fifth-grader," said Jordan.

Wait just a Nancy Drew minute. Was the green van back at school again? Were the bad guys training Mr Chips to steal chocolate-chip cookies now? But why? Maybe the cookies were just practice. Part of Mr Chips's training. Today they were teaching him to sniff out chocolate-chip cookies. Tomorrow – diamonds and jewels and stuff?

Nancy Drew was always vexed by her cases. Judy Moody was vexed *and* perplexed. Which was just a fancy-Nancy way of saying *stumped*.

Or was she?

"Jeepers! I think I've got it!" Judy cried. All she needed now was one more clue. One more piece to solve the puzzle and crack this case wide open. And that clue could only come from one person – postman Jack Frost.

The rest of the day, Judy Moody was on double-triple pins and needles. As soon as the bus dropped her off, she raced down the street to find Jack Frost.

"Hi, Jack Frost!" Judy called.

"So we're friends again?" Jack Frost teased.

"Chums," said Judy, nodding. "One question."

"Shoot," said Jack Frost.

"OK, think back to yesterday. Was

there anything else, anything in your lunch besides a corned beef sandwich?" Judy had her pad and pencil ready.

Jack Frost scratched his head. Jack Frost stroked his beard. "Well, let's see. There was a carrot..."

"Uh-huh, uh-huh. What else? What else?"

"A box of raisins..."

"AND?"

"Oh, yes. A super-scrumptious, ooey-gooey chocolate-chip cookie. I had my heart set on it, but all that was left were crumbs."

"Holy jeepers!" Judy screeched. At last, she, Judy Moody, had a break in the case. She knew just how Nancy Drew felt when she cracked the secret code, "Blue bells will be singing horses," in *Password to Larkspur Lane*.

The Case of
the Kissing Canine

Judy raced home to bake cookies. Before you could say I-spy-with-my-little-eye, flour was flying and butter was becoming batter.

"Do I smell chocolate-chip cookie dough?" Stink asked, peering into the bowl. "Sweet! Can I help?"

"Yeah, you can help by not eating all the chocolate chips. These are super-important detective cookies.

Find-Mr-Chips cookies. Crack-the-case cookies."

When the cookie sheets were full, Mum put the cookies in the oven for them.

"Stink, we're ready for Phase One. Go and get the fan," said Judy.

"The fan? What for?"

"We're going to set a trap. Since we can't seem to get to Mr Chips, we'll get him to come to us. With chocolate-chip cookies. Chocolate-chip cookies are the key to this case."

"You mean we'll blow the cookie smell outside and Mr Chips Super-Sniffer will sniff out the cookies and break free and come running?"

"Right into our arms," said Judy.

"Then the bad guys will come running after Mr Chips to catch him?"

"Right into Officer Kopp's arms," said Judy.

"Genius!" Stink said. Stink turned on the fan.

In no time, Judy and Stink heard a noise outside. They went running to the front door. It was Rocky and Frank.

"We thought you were Mr Chips!" said Judy. She explained her Master Catch-a-Thief Cookie Plan.

"How do you know it'll work?" asked Rocky.

"It worked on you, didn't it?" Judy said with a grin. "Time to call 1-800-MR-CHIPS and tell Officer Kopp to come quick if he wants to catch some bad guys."

"And tell him to bring backup," said Agent Pearl. "Just in case."

❧ ❧ ❧

Phase Two: Judy piled a mountain of hot-out-of-the-oven cookies on a plate. Rocky and Frank took some and made a trail of cookie crumbs leading down the pavement, around the corner, across the driveway and right up to the tent.

"If we don't catch Mr Chips, at least we'll catch a bunch of ants," said Stink. Stink always had ant farms on the brain.

"Stink, we'll hide in the tent with the rest of the cookies and wait for Mr Chips.

You take Frank's walkie-talkie and hide in the bushes at the front. If you see the green van, call us and say 'Chips ahoy!' That's the secret code."

"Cool beans," said Stink. "Wait a sec. Not fair. How come you guys get to be in the tent with cookies, and I have to be in the bushes all by myself without cookies?"

Judy held up the other walkie-talkie. "You can talkie to us any time you feel lonely."

Stink grabbed two cookies.

"Hey!" Judy barked. "Give those back."

"Rule Number One: never solve a crime on an empty stomach."

The Master Catch-a-Thief Cookie Trap was set. Now all they had to do was wait.

"Breaker, breaker, this is Adam-12," said Stink. "Do you copy me? We've got a possible Beetle Bailey."

"Huh?"

"It's a green VW Bug," said Stink.

"A Bug is not a van, Stink."

They watched and waited, waited and watched some more.

"Breaker, breaker," said Stink. "Come in, breaker. You read me?"

"Roger that," said Judy.

"Rocky's mum is taking out the rubbish. Over."

"Oops, I was supposed to do that," said Rocky.

"We've got an S-as-in-*Saturn*, Q-as-in-*quark*, U-as-in-*underwear*, I-as-in-*I-Don't-Know*, R-as-in-*rock*, E-as-in-*Easter-Bunny*, L-as-in-*loser*."

"A what?" Frank asked Judy.

"S-Q-U-I-R-E-L. I think he might mean *squirrel*. Learn to spell, Stink."

They waited some more.

"Beetle Bailey still parked. Cat burglar on a fence. Over," said Stink.

"Repeat. Did you say burglar?"

"It's just a cat."

"No green van?"

"Negative on the van. Just a crow picking at some leftover pizza on the road."

"So we just sit here?" asked Frank.

"My butt's asleep," said Rocky.

"Stakeouts are boring," Stink said over the walkie-talkie.

"NOT," said Judy. "This is as exciting as one time in *The Mystery of the Moss-Covered Mansion* when Nancy Drew chased a wild leopard and trapped him in the garage with a calm-down pill hidden inside a piece of meat."

"Chips ahoy! Chips ahoy!" crackled Stink. "Movement in bushes across the street. I think I see something furry."

Judy sat up, on alert. Frank and Rocky peered out of the tent flap.

"Negative. Scratch that. Just the cat burglar again."

Still more waiting.

"Chips ahoy!" Stink called again. "Got your ears on? I think I see a tail."

"A doggy tail?"

"False alarm. Just the *S-as-in-Saturn*. *Q-as-in—*"

"Stink, you have the right to remain silent," said Judy.

"Chips ahoy!" hissed Stink. "CHIPS AHOY!"

"He's like the boy who cried chips ahoy," said Frank.

"No way are we falling for that again." Just then, Judy heard a new sound. A sniffing, snuffling sound. A panting, pawing sound.

Is it? Was it? Could it be?

All three faces peered out of the front tent flap.

Holy jeepers! MR CHIPS!

Judy held out a cookie. "Good boy! Come here, Mr Chips."

In one leap, Mr Chips jumped right into the tent and on top of Judy, knocking her over. Cookies went flying. Mr Chips's tail was wagging five miles a minute. Judy hugged that wiggling ball of fur and kissed that puppy on his wet nose.

"Mr Chips!" said Rocky and Frank. "Who's a good boy? You are. Oh yes, you are!" Mr Chips rolled over, paws in the air. They tickled his tummy.

"Chips ahoy! Chips ahoy!" Stink was still yelling. "Come in, breaker. Do you read?" Finally, he came rushing into the tent, where the little brown furball was licking Judy, Rocky and Frank from head to toe.

"Told you!" Stink cried.

"Where'd you go, boy?" Rocky asked in between doggy kisses. "I wish you could tell us where you've been."

"You're safe from the bad guys now, Mr Chips," said Frank. "You didn't see the green van, did you, Stink?"

"Nope. Not even a piece of rope or a bite of corned beef sandwich."

"How'd you break away from those bad guys?" Judy asked. "Who's a smart doggy? You are."

"Breaker 1-9. We've got a bear coming. With a gumball machine."

"Stakeout's over, Stink. You can talk normally now," said Judy. Just then, she saw the black-and-white car that had pulled into the driveway, lights flashing.

"Officer Kopp!" she cried as he crossed the garden. "Look who we found!"

"Where did you get off to, boy?" Officer Kopp asked, snapping a lead on the puppy. Mr Chips leaped into Officer Kopp's arms, wagging his tail and licking him like he hadn't seen him in a year.

After all the How-Did-You's and Where-Have-You-Been's and Don't-Ever's, Officer Kopp asked, "So, how'd you find this guy?"

"Easy-peasy, lemon-squeezy," said Judy. "We set a chocolate-chip cookie trap."

"Good idea," said Officer Kopp.

"So did you bring backup?" Stink asked. "To catch the bad guys in the green van?"

"Yeah, we were on to them the day Mr Chips stole the dog bone from Speedy Market," said Frank.

"At first, we thought they were dog-nappers," said Judy.

"Yeah, like they took Mr Chips for reward money," Stink added.

"Then a Nancy Drew lightbulb went off in my head, and we followed a ton of clues all over town and figured out that they've been training Mr Chips to steal stuff. They're teaching him by making him sniff out chocolate-chip cookies."

"First it's cookies, then diamonds," said Stink.

Officer Kopp chuckled. "Hmm. That's some mighty interesting detective work, and you sure cracked the case. But I'm afraid there haven't been any reports at the police station about any diamonds going missing."

"See?" said Judy, turning to her fellow detectives. "Not only did we rescue Mr

Chips; we also stopped those bad guys in the nick of time."

"Yeah, looks to me like you caught the thief all right. The chocolate-chip cookie thief – our own Mr Chips."

Judy wasn't so sure. She, Eagle-Eye-Moody, was going to keep one eye peeled, just in case.

"We'll never know for sure, but I think Mr Chips is an escape artist – a regular Houdini. The best we can work out is that he pushed the bottom of the fencing just enough and squeezed out through a tiny opening. Then he ran all over town looking for food, he got so hungry."

"So that's why he stole a dog bone from Speedy Market?" asked Frank.

"And Jack Frost's corned beef sandwich!" said Stink.

"Then he got into the lunches at school and ate the chocolate-chip cookies," said Judy. "That's how he got the name Mr Chips. Because he loves chocolate-chip cookies. Am I right?"

"Not quite," said Officer Kopp. "Mr Chips doesn't *eat* chocolate-chip cookies. He buries them."

"Huh?" everybody asked.

"Most dogs have a sweet tooth. And they have a nose for chocolate. When Mr Chips first came home with me, my wife was baking chocolate-chip cookies. He went right for the chips and ate a handful before we could stop him."

"Oh no," said Frank. "Dogs aren't allowed to eat chocolate. It's like poison. It makes them sick."

"That's right," said Officer Kopp. "Poor guy was throwing up. We took him to the vet, and she told us that chocolate makes dogs sick. So before he even got any police-dog training, he was trained not to eat chocolate."

"Then why would he steal all those cookies?" Judy asked.

"Go ahead and give him a cookie," said Officer Kopp. "Watch what he does."

Judy held a cookie up to Mr Chips. He sniffed it, then ran with it between his teeth, the way he'd carried the egg across the stage at school that day.

He started digging under a tree.

"He's going to bury it!" Judy said. They ran after Mr Chips. Judy peered into the hole he had dug in the soft earth.

"Hey, there are loads of cookies in there," said Stink.

"Where'd he get those?" Rocky asked.

"He has a whole stash," Frank said, pointing and laughing.

"Thin Mints," said Judy. "Mum bought Girl Scout cookies from Jessica Finch, and I left some in the tent."

"What did I tell you?" said Officer Kopp. He scooped up Mr Chips. "Well, now that these super-detectives have found you, I'd better get you home, huh?"

He rubbed noses with Mr Chips. "I was worried I'd never see this guy again. I thank you, and Mr Chips thanks you."

"RARE!" said Judy. "I finally got to solve a mystery. The Mystery of the Missing Doggy Detective. This is just like the time Nancy Drew rescued a police-dog puppy in book No.1: *The Secret of the Old Clock*. No lie." She felt as shiny as the penny in Nancy Drew's penny loafers.

"Is there a reward?" Stink asked.

"Are you gonna arrest Mr Chips for stealing that dog bone?" Frank asked.

"Will Mr Chips still get to be a police dog?" Rocky asked.

"No, no, and yes," said Officer Kopp.

"But it'll be a while – he still has a lot to learn. A lot more training to do. Back to Doggy Detective School for you."

"Aw, I wish I could keep him," said Stink.

"Stink, he's not a pet," said Judy. "He's a crime buster. Aren't you, Mr Chips?" She rubbed noses with the puppy, too.

"Looks like this mystery's solved," said Officer Kopp. "No more cookie stealing for you, little fella. Case closed."

Case closed? If Judy Moody had learned one thing from Nancy Drew (besides Never Leave Home Without a Kirby Grip), it was that a detective's work was never done. Haunted houses. Secret diaries. Stolen diamonds. Around every corner was a mystery, just waiting to be solved. And where there was mystery, there would be Judy.

The kids waved to Officer Kopp and Mr Chips. "If any diamonds go missing," said Judy, "you know who to call."

"Who?" asked Stink.

"Judy Moody, Girl Detective," she said, grinning from ear to ear.

* CASE CLOSED *

photo by Michele McDonald

Megan McDonald is the author of the popular Judy Moody and Stink series, as well as the Judy Moody and Friends series for new readers. She has written many other books for children, including the Ant and Honey Bee stories, the Sisters Club series and several picture books. Before she began writing full-time, Megan McDonald worked as a librarian, a bookseller and a living-history actress. She lives in Northern California with her husband, Richard Haynes, who is also a writer.

Peter H. Reynolds is the illustrator of the popular Judy Moody and Stink series in addition to many other books, including several for which he is also author. They include his Creatrilogy of picture books: *The Dot, Ish,* and *Sky Colour.* His book *The Dot* has even inspired International Dot Day, which is celebrated around the world every September. Besides writing and illustrating, Peter H. Reynolds is a bookstore owner, animator and educator. He lives in Massachusetts with his family.

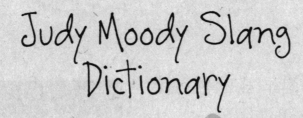

Judy Moody Slang Dictionary

From *double rare* to *star-spangled bananas*, here's a look at some of Judy Moody's favourite expressions. With this Judy Moody slang dictionary, you'll never be at a loss for words – and that's definitely double cool!

rare!: cool!

double rare!: way cool!

double cool!: twice as cool!

ROAR!: what to say when you're angry or frustrated

pizza table: the little plastic piece that keeps a pizza from touching the top of the pizza box

bothers: little brothers who bother you all the time!

smad: sad and mad, at the same time!

same-same: what you say when you and your friend do something that's the same

phoney baloney: fake

not-boring: interesting

boing!: aha!

star-spangled bananas!: what you say when you're surprised or amazed

L.B.S: Long Boring Story

Ouch Face: the face you make when someone's pulling your hair

ABC gum: Already Been Chewed gum

nark: bad mood

T. P. Club: the Toad Pee Club

oogley: gross

caterpillar eyebrow: the way your eyebrows look when you're in a mood (not a good mood, a bad mood!)

or something: what you say when someone presents you with a list of choices that end with "or something" and you don't agree with any of the choices

V.I.Q: Very Important Question

Antarctica: the desk at the back of Mr Todd's classroom where you have to sit if you're causing trouble

goopy: cheesy

IN THE MOOD FOR MORE JUDY MOODY? THEN TRY THESE!

MEGAN McDONALD
illustrated by Peter H. Reynolds
JUDY MOODY
AROUND THE WORLD IN 8½ DAYS
Ciao!

MEGAN McDONALD
illustrated by Peter H. Reynolds
JUDY MOODY GOES TO COLLEGE
Genius!

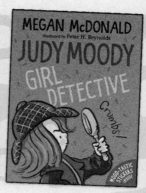

MEGAN McDONALD
illustrated by Peter H. Reynolds
JUDY MOODY GIRL DETECTIVE
Crumbs!

MEGAN McDONALD
illustrated by Peter H. Reynolds
JUDY MOODY AND THE NOT BUMMER SUMMER
Thrill-a-delic!
BIG FOOT CLUB

MEGAN McDONALD
illustrated by Peter H. Reynolds
JUDY MOODY AND THE BAD LUCK CHARM
whoa!

MEGAN McDONALD
illustrated by Peter H. Reynolds
JUDY MOODY MOOD MARTIAN
Loop-de-loop!

MEGAN McDONALD
illustrated by Peter H. Reynolds
JUDY MOODY AND THE BUCKET LIST
1-2-3, whee!

MEGAN McDONALD
illustrated by Peter H. Reynolds
JUDY MOODY AND THE RIGHT ROYAL TEA PARTY

Have
you
met
STINK?

Meet Stink, Judy Moody's little "bother,"
er, brother. <u>Very</u> little brother...

Stink was short. Short, shorter, shortest.
Stink was an inchworm. Short as a ...
stinkbug!

Stink was the shortest one in the
Moody family (except for Mouse, the cat).
The shortest second-grader in Class 2D.
Probably the shortest human being in the
whole world, *including Alaska and Hawaii.*
Stink was one whole head shorter than
his sister, Judy Moody. Every morning
he made Judy measure him. And every
morning it was the same.

One metre, twelve centimetres tall.
Shrimpsville.

Excerpt from *Stink: The Incredible Shrinking Kid*

MEET JUDY MOODY'S BROTHER STINK!

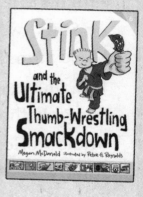